# PORTSMOUTH ISLAND

## Short Stories & History

*2004 Limited Edition*

## By Dot Salter Willis and Ben B. Salter

### Editing by Frances A. Eubanks and Lynn S. Salsi

DEDICATION:
This limited first edition was published to honor Ben B. Salter and Dot Salter Willis.

INTRODUCTION:

It was an honor to edit this special edition of *Portsmouth Island Short Stories and History.* This new version was conceived as a commemorative edition for the 250th anniversary celebration which took place on April 17, 2004, at the biannual Portsmouth Island Reunion. It is a tribute to the island and the brave seafaring people who lived there. Most of all, this is to honor Dot Salter Willis. She has kept many stories of Portsmouth Island alive through her book that was first published in 1972. Dot has spent many years helping to save the history of Portsmouth through her efforts with the Friends of Portsmouth Island. Everyone looks forward to Dot's presentation of the Portsmouth history at the reunion.

We would like to thank Cindi Hamilton of the Carteret County Historical Society for her encouragement and Janet S. Metcalfe of Montville Publications for the book's cover and overall design.

We hope that you will enjoy this book and will visit Portsmouth often.

Frances A. Eubanks
Lynn S. Salsi
April 2004

ISBN: 0-9706527-2-0

Portsmouth Island                                    Short Stories & History

# Table of Contents

## Dot Salter Willis

Dot was born on Portsmouth Island, the second of five children of Ben and Thelma Styron Salter. She lived on the island next door to her grandparents and attended the island school. When she was seven, her family moved to Atlantic, North Carolina and after a few years they moved back to Portsmouth.

*Dot Salter Willis*
*(Photo by Francies Eubanks)*

Dot and her father shared a love of the island. She recorded her father's memories and compiled them into this book as a seventy-third birthday gift in 1972.

This is the story of Portsmouth Island told by Dot and her father. They were born on the island and lived there. Both were eye-witnesses to the history of a very special place.

## Frances A. Eubanks

Frances' photographs have been featured in books museums, touring shows, newspapers, and magazine covers. She has received many awards including the Willie Parker Peace History Book award, and the Paul Green Multi Media award. She received the 2003 President's award from the North Carolina Society of Historians. Frances is a founding member, former president, and board member of the Friends of Portsmouth Island. She traces her heritage through the Salter family who lived on the island from the 1770s until 1959. Her grandparents, mother, aunt and uncle were born on the island. During her youth she spent holidays and summers visiting her relatives.

## Lynn S. Salsi

Lynn is dedicated to recording North Carolina history in children's books, non-fiction, and historical novels. Her plays for children have been produced throughout the southeast, New York, Baltimore, London England, Portsmouth, England, and Edinburgh, Scotland. She is well known for enrichment presentation in schools and colleges and is a speaker for the North Carolina Humanities Council Speakers forum. She enjoys viewing history through the eyes of those who have lived it. Among her writing awards are the American Library Association Notable Book award, the Bill Smith Magazine Writing award, the Willie Parker Peace History Book award, and the Paul Green Multi Media award. She was named the 2001 Historian of the Year by the North Carolina Society of Historians.

## Benjamin Bowden Salter

I was born on Portsmouth Island, North Carolina on June 30, 1899, the oldest son of John Wallace Salter and Sidney Styron Salter. I had four sisters and four brothers.

I attended grammar school in the one room schoolhouse on the island. At the age of fifteen, I left home to find work. My first job was as a deck hand on the on the S. S. Jamestown, Old Dominion Steamship Company, Norfolk, Virginia.

*Benjamin Bowden Salter*
*(Photo by Francies Eubanks)*

At the age of eighteen, I met and married Thelma Styron, age seventeen, the daughter of William Reilly and Lydia Ann Emory Styron. We are the parents of five girls and one boy; Ethel Marie, Doris Evelyn, Mary Elizabeth, Geraldine Farrar,

Margaret Carolyn, and William Benjamin. Doris Evelyn was the only one of our children born on the island.

I was in the United States Coast Guard for a short while stationed in New York State. Then I was engaged in the fish business in Pamlico County for quite some time. But most of my life, I have been a commercial fisherman and guide for hunters.

Throughout all of these years, I have from time to time returned to Portsmouth Island the place of my birth, which I love dearly. At this time, my wife and I live in Atlantic, North Carolina. Thelma and I celebrated our fiftieth wedding anniversary on Sunday, July 16, 1967.

*(Ed. note - written by Ben Salter for his daughter, Dot, in 1972.)*

# My Home on the Island

I was born in was an eight room, two story house, painted white. The furniture was early American, as most of it was hand made. The kitchen and dining area was one large room. The long dining table was in one end of the room. I remember the many people that sat down to eat at that table with my mama and papa and us children.

Our home was open to receive anyone who needed shelter or wanted to spend the night or week. Our friends would come from the mainland and spend weeks at the time; we enjoyed having them.

The house was built with large gables in the end of the upper story. There were two large windows where my mama and us children would go to see the boats and ships at sea and in the sound. Mama went there to look for papa when it looked as if a storm was coming up. We kept a pair of binoculars in the window so we could see far off on the ocean or sound.

In 1907, when the *John I. Snow* came ashore, papa bought the large white columns to put on the front porch, four of

*Crissie and Manson Fulcher - Crissie was the island midwife. (Photo courtsey of Dot S. Willis private collection.)*

them. This made our home look real pretty to me. There are lots of folks that remember that house and the many good times we had there. It was a gathering place for the young folks in those days. Mama would let us roll up the rug and have dances in the front room.

After my sister Pearl was married, she moved to New Bern. She and her husband Jerome would come back home for Christmas. We would decorate the house and have a big party. I get home sick just thinking about the good times and our home of long ago.

I married Thelma and we lived next door to mama and papa. It was a small four room house, built about six steps off the ground, so that the water would not go inside when the storms came. We were happy there.

When it came time for our first child to be born, my wife went to stay with her parents on Hog Island. My first daughter was born there. My second daughter, Dot, was born in our home on Portsmouth. She loves the island and enjoys going back there. She can remember when she lived there as a child.

After so many storms hit the island, most of the people started to move away. Mama and papa moved to Atlantic after the hurricane of '33. Then Thelma and I moved there, too. We sold our house; it was later moved down the banks.

The stone steps from mama's and papa's house can still be seen. I go there and sit and think about the good times we once had in the house and on the island.

# The Island That is Slowly Disappearing

Portsmouth Island, North Carolina, was first settled by white people in the year 1700. Before then, it was called "Croatan," home of the Indians. Portsmouth was established as a town in the year 1753 by an act of the North Carolina General Assembly. John Kersey was the first owner. It was laid out in one-half acre lots. Mr. John Tolson bought the first lot in 1756, for twenty shillings.

Portsmouth was once a thriving sea port town, the most beautiful of all the islands on the outer banks. Most of the first settlers came from England; the people still have an old English brogue. In 1846, there was a Federal Hospital, two churches, a school, an academy, customhouse, Naval stores, three or four privately owned stores, and even back then, a barroom.

At one time, many ships came into the Ocracoke inlet between Portsmouth and Ocracoke Island. Portsmouth was the chief seaport along the Atlantic Outer Banks. Boats from Norfolk, Virginia; Washington, North Carolina; Morehead City, Beaufort, Elizabeth City, New Bern and other towns arrived daily to off load and pick up cargo.

Portsmouth had many nice homes located all along the island that was five miles long. The houses were so pretty painted white with all the green grass just like a carpet and the white sand all around. Most of the homes on Portsmouth were large ones, which were kept nice and clean. The people had small houses built in the side or back yard to cook in, this was a kitchen and dining room. Here they would cook their fish, so their big house would not be scented and hot in the summer. They also had what people in those days called a milk house in their yards to put their food in, so it would stay cool in the summer. Everything on the island was so clean. I have been told that a man could wear a white shirt for a week without getting it soiled, for there was no dust and dirt.

The good folks on Portsmouth always opened their homes to everyone. People who came to the island always felt welcome and wanted to return. I wish everyone could have seen this island as I did when I was a boy.

Families by the name of Wallace, Blount, Dixon, Gilgo, Styron, Daly, Roberts, Robinson, Babb, Nelson, Mason, Tolson, Kersey, Williams, McWilliams, Salter, Willis, Pigott, and many others lived on Portsmouth Island. After so many storms, the people started to move away. Their homes were destroyed or torn down and moved to the mainland. Some of their homes were sold to other people for hunting or fishing camps. A few of the old structures still stand.

When I was a boy, a man could walk from Portsmouth to Cape Lookout on dry land. Today you have to go by boat with four inlets to cross.

Most of our family members are now living in Atlantic and New Bern, North Carolina. The Roberts moved to Oriental, North Carolina, the Robinsons, Nelsons, and Masons to Atlantic. The Babbs moved to Norfolk, Virginia and Beaufort, North Carolina. Other families settled in other towns on the coast. Portsmouth Island people were spread to other places. Not many families stayed on the island.

Only three people have their homes on the island now, Henry Pigott, Elma Dixon, and Marion Gray Babb (Mrs. Lillian Babb's daughter). These people do not stay there year round. They live on the mainland in the winter time.

Portsmouth Island had people, ponies, cattle, sheep, hogs, and plenty of grazing land. All the livestock and most all of the people are long gone from this island that is so dear to my heart. It is slowly disappearing into the sea. At this time, it is only a narrow strip of beach from the sound to the sea. The most beautiful and most thriving of all the islands on the outer banks, that was so well populated at one time and such a nice place for people to live and raise their families is just a memory to the folks that lived there and loved it so well.

*Ben Salter and Ed Dixon at age 19.*
*(Photo courtesy of Dot S. Willis private collection)*

# The Island of Long Ago

Portsmouth Island in the late 1700s and early 1800s was a beautiful place, (I was told). It was a town with roads, houses, stores, and a hospital. The old folks talked about how the middle of the island was a forest. People used to cut the trees and carry them to the mainland to have them sawed into lumber. Then brought the wood back to build their homes.

I have been told that grapes were so plentiful on the island that people would come in their "yard boats" up the Coast Guard Creek and sit on the side of the boat and pick grapes that hung over the water.

I remember when there were large trees, so that we could climb high up in them and watch the ships at sea. Water did not cover the beach like it does today, only in bad storms.

You used to be able to walk from the larger community of Portsmouth to the Sheep Island end. It was all dry land with just one bridge to cross at what we called the "big bushes." There were houses all along the way down the banks and we knew all of the people.

The road, called the Straight Road, stretched from one end of the island to the other. It was wide enough for a horse and cart. There had always been horses on Portsmouth Island, as well as cattle and sheep, too. The livestock was all removed after the fence law was passed.

People used to fence in the yards around their houses because horses and cattle roamed free on the island. They fed wherever they could. Since the yards were all covered with grass and flowers and fruit trees all the way back through the 1800s, most of the houses had a pretty picket fence. In the original community of Portsmouth, the land was laid off in one-half acre lots in the 1700s. Those who bought a lot had to build a substantial structure on it within a year.

Since I was not born until 1899, I can't remember back before the early 1900s. But when I was a boy, things were a lot different than they are today. There were no large stagnated ponds like today. There was no slew or creek cut across the beach. You could see from house to house and walk wherever you wanted to go or ride your horse.

The Coast Guard Station first served as the Life Saving Station and was built a few years before I was born. It was painted white with a cement walkway all around it and had a walk leading to every building. The men stationed there all lived around the station in little white houses.

The larger houses on the island had what people called a "widow's walk." It was a structure built all around the upper story so the residents could walk all around and look for ships at sea or boats in the sound.

In the 1700s and 1800s, there were Indians on Portsmouth. Some of the people that are descendents of Portsmouth people were part Indian. It showed in their faces – high cheek bones, olive skin, dark brown eyes and straight black hair.

After the Federal Hospital was closed, it was turned into a telegraph office and recreation hall. The people used to have square dances there. People would come from Cedar Island and Ocracoke to these dances. I am told that my Uncle Dave Salter was a good dancer. He was so light on his feet that he really could move them fast. He was quite a ladies' man and loved to dress up in a suit and white shirt. When he passed away, Miss Sophie said, "Dave's dancing feet have stopped."

People enjoyed themselves better in those days.

# My Life on Portsmouth
### By Dot Salter Willis

I was born at home on the island on January 13, 1921. Mrs. Chrissie Fulcher was the island's midwife and she delivered me. I was told that it was a cold day. Of course, I don't remember. Our house was in the area called Sheep Island. It was all part of Portsmouth, but it was a section at the lower end and was not a separate island. It got the name because one of the early residents was a man who kept a lot of sheep. When it was stormy and bad, a gully would come up from the creek and water would run across the area. That's the only time the area was like an island.

As I grew older, my sister, Ethel Marie, and I had a lot of fun playing around our home. There was no one to hurt us. We only had roaming horses and cattle to be afraid of. I called Ethel Marie "Sister." She was three years older, but she was small for her age and we looked almost like twins.

We ran back and forth from our home to grandma's house next door. Aunt Jenny (Virginia Laughinghouse) was always there and we loved to stay with her. She was about ten years older than Sister, so she seemed more like an older sister than an aunt. She told me that she carried me around on her hip when I was a baby. We missed her when she moved to Atlantic to go to business school. But Jenny came back to visit Portsmouth as long as grandmother lived there.

We knew everyone and visiting was a big part of our life. Mr. Ed and Mrs. Kate Styron lived across the road from us. They would come over to our house sometime after dark carrying a little kerosene lantern. They came to hear my mother read continuous stories. She was a good reader and would sit and read Zane Gray and all that kind of thing to us. The adults would sit in the front room, while the children played on the floor. One house down a little way was Sissie Annie Ricci and her son, Allie. We called her Sissie, she was my grandmother Sidney's sister.

We could go across the creek or down the road to Uncle Dave Salter's house (my grandfather's brother). We ran in and out of his house as if it was our own. He would catch us and hug us. He loved us almost as well as our grandpa. Not far down the lane from our uncle lived Aunt Sabra Roberts and Cousin Nora. Nora married Harris Fulcher, Uncle Jerome's brother. They had three daughter, Lucille, Lena, and Sabra Elizabeth. I can only remember knowing Lucille while on Portsmouth. Cousin Norwood, Nora's brother and his wife Ruth, lived on the island for awhile. They had four children. I played with Elton and Estell. Elton is in Oriental and Estelle lives in Atlantic.

We would walk down the banks to the store and to the post office with mama; sometimes daddy would go with us too. It was quite a long walk for two little girls, Mama would stop with us along the way to see some of the island people and so we could rest.

We always stopped to see Mrs. Mattie Gilgo. She lived on the island with her four children. Ethel, her daughter, and Donald, her youngest son was about our age so we played with them. We loved to go there. Mr. Lemmie Gilgo and his wife and children lived not too far from them. We would stop there also and stay a little while, then we'd go on.

Down the banks, we went to see Uncle Theodore and Aunt Annie Salter. They lived in a large two-story house near the haul over almost to the end of the island. Uncle Theodore ran a little store and there was a walled off area in the front corner for the post office. Aunt Annie was the Portsmouth postmaster. They had one son and thee daughters, Mable, Ernest, Clara Belle, and Dorothy Mae. Clara and Dorothy Mae were the age of my sister and I. We had a lot of fun going up and down the road and playing together. Sometimes Aunt

Annie, Uncle Theodore, and their children would come to visit us.

Sometimes we went to see Mrs. Sarah Styron and her daughter, Dorothy Louise, she was my age too. My full name is Doris Evelyn, Uncle Dave called me "Dot." So, we had three Dot's on Portsmouth Island all the same age. We were all very good friends.

We all liked to visit Lizzie and Henry Pigott over on Doctor's Creek. Lizzie cut our hair when we were little. They were brother and sister and had a pretty home with a white picket fence all around. Everything was neat and clean inside and outside. My sister liked to climb on Lizzie's fence. Just as Lizzie said, "Ethel Marie, you are going to fall." She fell and skinned both of her legs real bad.

Miss Elma Dixon lived over by the church. Next door was Mrs. Lillian Babb and Mr. Jess Babb. They had three daughters, Edna Earl, Jesse Lee, and Marian Gray. Since they were our age, we went to see them. There were a lot of children on Portsmouth.

Aunt Neva and Uncle Sam Williams lived down the road by the Coast Guard Station. Uncle Sam was in the Coast Guard. He would put me on one of the large Coast Guard horses and then he'd lead the horse around. Sometimes he would take some of us for a ride. He even took the horse-drawn cart and carried us back home. Uncle Sam and Aunt Neva had three children. I played with the two oldest, Johnny Ervin and Eula Pearl. They were a little younger than me. Later, they had a son named Roger Darrell.

We used to play up and down the beach where we made large sand castles and had the best time. We'd find pieces of window glass, plates, cups, and saucers in the sand. We used the pieces of glass and crockery to draw off a house in the beach sand. We'd draw off a big space and say, "This is the living room or this is the kitchen. Then we'd draw off the front of the house and make places for doors and windows. We didn't have a lot of play toys, but we liked to play house. When I asked Daddy how all the broken dishes could be so close to the beach, he said that houses used to be there, but over the years they'd washed away during storms.

On the way home, the cattle would get after us sometimes and we'd run home as fast as our legs could carry us. We were scared of those large bulls. We liked to play outside around our house and around our grandparent's house. When we were a little older we took bricks and built an outside furnace. We'd build up the bricks and use it to bake potatoes in the coals of a fire.

I went to school on the island with all of the other children. It was a one-room school house. The building was located about middle way of the island. My teacher was Mrs. Mary Dixon. She had a son named Felts and a daughter named Bethania.

We could walk the Straight Road to school, but we liked to walk close to the beach on the sandy sand (not on the ocean) and then cut across over to school. As we were walking we liked to pull the sour grass. We folded it up and put it in our mouths and chewed it like chewing gum. It had a sweet yet sour taste that we liked. If it had little tiny nuts on it, we'd carefully pull the nuts up and eat them. They tasted a little like peanut butter. We all carried our lunch to school. At lunch time we sat out on the grass in warm weather and ate together. We did not have much to carry in those days. I took a bottle of water and a cold biscuit with a streak of lean/a streak of fat. It was usually combined with an egg. I ate so many egg sandwiches that I can hardly eat an egg now.

I think back and long for things to be as they were then. We had no worries about children getting into trouble like they do today.

I remember my daddy, Uncle Tom, and Uncle Charlie rounding up the young horses to brand. Then they'd break the wild ones so they could ride them. Uncle Ross and David were there too.

I was still young when we moved from the island the first time. But we moved back several times. I don't think daddy could stand not being there. Grandmother and granddaddy moved away after the '33 storm. That's when the ocean and the sound met over the island. Uncle David said that the water was under his armpits in the front room of his house. After the storm was over, he said that horses and cattle were laying around drowned and that the fence was full of dead chickens.

Years have gone by, but my memories are happy ones. I love the island and all of the people who lived there. Our family still goes back from time to time.

*The Straight Road was a horse and cart road that was cleared in the 1700's. It runs the entire length of the island, begining at Haulover Point, runs through Middle Settlement and to Sheep Island.*

# Hunting on the Island

Portsmouth was once a wonderful place to hunt wild fowl. Many geese and ducks came every winter to this island. When I was a boy, my father took out hunters. Our home was always filled with men going hunting. We would get up real early in the morning, mama would cook us a good breakfast, and we would all start out on a hunting trip. My brothers and I would help our father fit the hunters out. Our hunting lodge was called, "The Salter Gun Club."

Redhead ducks would light on the water. There were so many they would look like an island. Geese would fly over in big flocks and light close by. Boy would those hunters have fun shooting them.

My father would shoot them sometimes for market. He shipped geese, ducks, and brandt by the "sugar barrel" full, and sold them to a man up north. At that time, they made decorations for women's hats out of the plumage. I remember well the song that came out about that time, "The Bird on Nellie's Hat".

Many men came to hunt with the Salters. Babe Ruth, the famous ball player, came down one time. After that, we named one of our blinds after him, the "Babe Ruth" blind. Now, you might wonder what a blind is. Well it is a kind of wooden box built on poles out in the water, where hunters can hide from the fowl. It blocks the fowl from seeing the hunter(s) and then they can shoot the ducks and geese.

Mr. Jodie Styron and Mr. Tom Bragg, old friends of ours, ran a good hunting lodge for many years also. They lived on the upper part of the island. They worked together for many years when the fowl were plentiful, Some people still have hunting camps on the island and go there from time to time to hunt.

I still have a hunting lodge there where my friends and family sometimes go to hunt, fish, or just to get away from it all. We still enjoy our times on Portsmouth, hunting, fishing, or just sitting around talking about the old days long before my hair turned gray.

I love to go there to just look around and reminisce. There are no telephones, nor televisions. There's just peace and quiet. It is the most wonderful place to go for a nice long rest away from the hustle and bustle of the towns and people.

## Fishing

*The Salter Boys (l. to r.) Charlie, Tom, Ben. They enjoyed fishing together.*
*(Photo courtesy of Dot Salter Willis private collection.)*

Fish were plentiful in the waters around Portsmouth Island. My father, my brother Tom, and I would fish together; sometimes we would fish pound nets. The nets would have to be tarred in cold tar. Setting them in hot sun would almost blister a man. We would change nets twice a week. That means, we'd take up a dirty net and put down a clean one. If the nets set out too long, they would have so much grass and barnacles in them that they would be too heavy to catch fish.

Once we caught a saw fish; it was the first one I ever saw. We had a hard time getting him. His saw was a prize; it was five feet, six inches long.

I remember catching so many mullets that our nets would not hold them. Our nets would not hold the fish and I remember how pretty they were when we brought them to the top of the water. Then sometimes we would go fishing and come home without a fish. That's the "Fisherman's life."

One day in July 1960, I went with my brothers Tom and Charlie and a good friend of ours, Alvin Harris, from Atlantic to Portmouth for mullet fishing. We caught a lot of pretty mullet the first two days of the week. On the third day, we started to go fishing and a bad thunder squall came up. We took shelter on the upper end of the island where my brother Charlie was killed by lightning. That was a sad day for the Salters and their friends.

My Uncle Dave Salter bought the first engine that ever came to Portsmouth Island. It was a three-horse power Palmer. He put the engine in a large pound net boat. Folks in those days called the boats, "skiffs." He thought a three-horse power engine was large enough to drive a steamship. People came from all over the island to see the engine. It wasn't long before everyone had engines in their fishing boats.

The island folks would salt fish to eat in the winter in order to have food when it was too cold to fish. Some would salt extra to sell, as it seems that lots of folks liked salt fish and sweet potatoes in the wintertime. The water around Portsmouth was pretty at night. We went mullet fishing or floundering at night and we'd catch a boatload of fish.

I have a friend, Mr. Walt Nelson from Atlantic, that would come to Portsmouth to catch flounder. He sure could catch them. Mr. Walt was called the "flounder king". He caught enough flounder that he made a living and raised a large family.

In 1919, Mr. Charlie Wallace and Will Webb started a project, a large fish factory to make fertilizer and then save the oil. This was to be a large factory. They hired a man by the name of Wilson to drive the well to get fresh water. My brother, Tom, and a colored man by the name of Morris Fulford helped him. They worked many weeks to get fresh water. At last, they hit an overflow at the depth of 595 feet. The factory was built on Casey's Point at the cost of $110,000.00.

# Oystering

Lots of people on Portsmouth Island made their living in the winter by oystering. There were plenty of oysters on the rocks and shoals around the sound side of the island.

Many tubs of oysters and clams were caught and sent by boat to the mainland to market. Oysters were so plentiful that they were hauled by boat, bushels and bushels of oysters to be planted in other waters up and down the coast.

People would come from miles around to catch the Portsmouth oysters they were the best they would say. I think they are the best tasting oysters in the world and I have eaten oysters from Portsmouth Island to Long Island Sound, New York.

There were more oysters around Portsmouth Island than any place I know. On the south side of Wallace's Channel, there were fourteen oyster rocks that yielded from ten to fifty thousand bushels of oysters every year. In those days, folks could make a good living selling oysters in the winter.

Now the oysters are disappearing from the waters around Portsmouth Island. Today, in 1970, there are not three bushels of oysters on those same rocks. The few that can be found are still the best oysters around these parts.

Today is March 2nd, 1959, a bad day. The wind is out of the north and it is raining. The tide is high; I have seen many days like this on Portsmouth Island. It is a good time to shoot ducks and geese from shore blinds. On days like this in the winter, I have seen wild geese light in the goose pound (pen) with my papa's tame geese.

We used to have live decoys for hunting. My father had lots of them. We had 90 head of geese at one time. Papa used to buy and sell them in the fall of the year.

# Tame Geese

Everyone that owned geese would get together in the fall and pen them. One day, papa told me to go with Mr. George Gilgo to drive the geese. I was glad to go with him as I liked him very much. They had penned the geese abut the last of September. There were lots of them because the old geese that they turned out in the spring laid eggs. When they hatched, one goose might have as many as six or seven goslings.

I remember once that my Uncle Warren Gilgo had a goose setting on some eggs. Her nest was on a small island in the middle of the creek. Joe and Jesse Babb and I were going to the store for groceries, when I said to Joe, "Do you want to see something pretty?" Of course, he said, "Yes." I told him to go over on the little island and he would see it. I told him that the goose had the prettiest little goslings he had ever seen.

Joe did not know that an old gander would fight for his goose and young ones. He got almost there and sure enough, the gander came at him just as mad as he could in a boat, right over where the large rock was. He caught Joe by the seat of his pants and all the while the goose flapped his wings as hard as he could. Joe began to run, then he would fall down and that gander would catch him again. He sure gave Joe a good beating. After awhile, Joe got away from the bird. The gander went back to the goose and goslings. As long as Joe lived he never went to look at another goose nest.

Today there are no more tame geese on the island. A federal law was passed saying that we could no longer use live decoys. Papa and us boys got rid of most of them. We sold some and the storms took lots of them away.

I do not think that there is a man living that knew more

about geese than Mr. George Gilgo. He knew some by their honk. One day, we were penning geese and one honked way off. Mr. George said, "Ben, that is the gander I got from your papa," and sure enough it was. One thing I do know, you have to live around geese a long time to know them by their honk. Some folks could stay around them a lifetime and never know one from the other.

A wild Canada goose will not lay and hatch in the area. Brant will not lay around Portsmouth either. Swan Island used to be a good place where mallard ducks, black ducks, and the green-head mallard laid their eggs. I have also seen black ducks with their little ones around Raccoon Island.

When I was a boy, there was a large rock island about five or six miles out in the sound off Portsmouth Island. This rock island had trees growing on it, the name of the rock was Royal Shoal Rock. Thousands of sea gulls and pelicans laid their eggs on the sand there; then they sat on them until they hatched. When they came off their nest you could see the most little birds running around on that island. Today, there is no rock. You can go over the place.

# Pony Penning Bankers

Lee Daniels. One day, he called me at the Portsmouth Island Station from the Core Banks Station and asked me to go to Atlantic to get a horse and take her to Hatteras Island. Lee had traded horses with Mr. Midgett from Avon, North Carolina. It was a long way to go along the coast, but I did this for my friend. I also enjoyed riding.

Now, this horse was a fast and nervous one. She would paw and kick at every chance. In those days, there were no inlets to cross between Portsmouth and Core banks where Atlantic was located. But I would have to cross both the Ocracoke and Hatteras Inlets. I took my saddle and bridle and went by mailboat to Atlantic to Lee's father's home. Harvey Daniels, Lee's brother, had kept the horse in a stable for about two months. He had fed her, and just let her stay in the sable, because everyone was afraid to ride her. When I took her out, she was wild as a deer. We took her by boat to the Core Banks When I was a boy, ponies ran wild on the island. I was

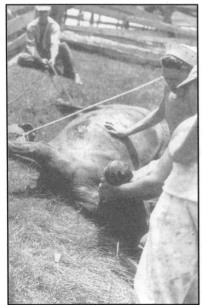

told that ponies were on the island when the first white man settled there. Some of them came from ships that came ashore on the beach. As they interbred, they were a little bigger than the small ponies seen around the mainland these days. They are called "banker ponies." They were beautiful as they ran free on the island.

My father, my brothers, and I had quite a few ponies. Each year the people that owned the ponies would have a round-up. We called it a penning. We made a big corral and ran the ponies into it. Then we got the colts and branded them. Every man had his own brand, it was hard work, but we enjoyed it so much.

People from the mainland would come to see the ponies penned. The people that owned them sold some. After the sale, they would have to move them to the mainland by boat. This was quite a trip for man and beast.

My brothers and I would have such a good time breaking the ponies so we could ride. The next year, we could use these ponies to round up the wild ones. Many times, my mother would say, "You boys are going to be killed." We took many falls and had narrow escapes, but we never got seriously hurt.

Let me tell you about an experience I had one day.

I had a friend that was in the Coast Guard Station at Core Banks. His name was Lester Station near the Cape Lookout lighthouse. At that time, the officer in charge was Fred Gillikin. He said that he would hold her until I could saddle and bridle her, so he sat on a fence and held her by the halter.

A man by the name of Warren Alligood was there to haul wood from a barge into the station to be used for heating and cooking. He said we would go along together to Portsmouth, but when Captain Fred turned the horse loose, I never saw Warren again. I rode along the high water mark just as fast as that horse could go. We reached Portsmouth, a distance of thirty one miles in about two and one half hours. I put the horse in the Portsmouth Coast Guard Station pound until the next morning.

Uncle Theodore Salter and Ed Dixon, a friend (now retired from the Coast Guard and living on Harkers Island) helped me take the horse over to Ocracoke island. We did this by small boat. We tied the horse by the side of the boat and she would walk or run when she could where the water was shallow. She swam the rest of the way. The boys on Ocracoke Island had some fast ponies. When they heard that I was coming on a fast horse, they wanted race.

They were waiting for me when I reached the shore. I said, "Boys, this horse is worn out, I can't race now." But they wanted to see the horse run. After such a trip across the inlet I thought that she would not run anyway. I got on her and just let her go. When we went into the woods, we left those boys far behind. I stopped by Mr. Gary Bragg's home for water and got water for the horse. Then we went to the Hatteras Inlet Station. Just as we got to the "great swash" the wind changed and it began to blow hard. The tide began to rise, but I made it and put the horse in the pound there. The weather was so bad I had to stay at the Hatteras Coast Guard Station for three days. On the third day, the sun rose and the weather was calm. Before I left, I had breakfast with my friends at the station, Willie Gaskins said the blessing or prayer. He said, "Dear Lord, thanks for all of the food we have." Then he named it all by name. At the close, he said, "Lord, bless Ben and never let him come here again. Amen." He made it all rhyme.

So you see, I loved to ride. It was so nice when a group of young people would get together and ride their horses along the beach on moonlit nights. The young people on Portsmouth Island did not have many things to do, but this was one of the things we enjoyed most.

# Caught in a Storm

On August 9, 1924, I had been to Atlantic, NC where we were living. My third daughter, Mary Elizabeth, was born on this day. After making sure that my wife, Thelma and new daughter were going to be all right, I started to return to Portsmouth to go fishing as I was doing this for a living. I did not like to leave them so soon, but I needed to go back to fish my nets that were in the water.

I took my boat and supplies and started toward Portsmouth. In those days, we did not have speed boats. It took about two and a half hours to go from Atlantic to Portsmouth.

The wind was to the southeast and was squally. But the hawlers had gone out fishing, so I thought the weather was ok to make the trip.

A few days before, I had replenished my fuel supply, but unknown to me, someone had borrowed most of it. I did not know this until I was well on my way. I noticed that I was low when I reached Harbor Island and stopped off to get some from Ferrin Willis. He and his family were taking care of the club house there. They wanted me to spend the night with them, but I thought that I could make Portsmouth before dark, so I decided to go on.

When I got to the Evergreen slew or Three Hat Channel, I gave completely out of gas. I anchored my boat, put up two sets of colors to an 18 foot pole. I could see the Portsmouth Coast Guard Station at times. At other times, I couldn't see anything, as it began to rain and blow hard.

The mail boat from Morehead City named the *Ocracoke* captained by Gus Nelson with mate Will Willis, was due to pass about four o'clock on the way to Ocracoke Island. I thought they would see me, but they did not. I could see them, but they did not see me.  My last hope of being seen was gone unless the men at the Coast Guard Station spotted me.

It began to blow harder and about dark the wind changed to the Northeast.  The men at the station did not see me.  I had to cut my anchor loose to keep from sinking my boat.  She drifted off with the wind and the sea.  I drifted for some time baling water out of the boat as hard as I could.  By this time, I couldn't see land or anything, as it was dark and very stormy.  I thought that I was going to be washed into the

*Ben B. Salter, working at his net spreads. He worked as a commercial fisherman and hunting guide.* (Photo courtesy Dot Walter Willis private collection)

ocean, the foxfire from the waves was high and light. It seemed as if I drifted for miles and miles. I was afraid. Late that night, or early in the morning, I struck land. By then, it was light enough that I could tell where I was. I was on the highest part of the Myrtle Hammock about eight miles from Portsmouth island. After it got light good, I began to walk toward Portsmouth. It was a long walk, but I made it. My Mama and Papa had not moved from the island, at this time. Mama was so glad to see me that she cried. She was afraid that I had been drowned during the night. The tide had been nine inches deep in our house during the night.

I went down to the Coast Guard Station to get the men to help me get my boat off the beach, which they did later.

Mr. Mason Nelson from Atlantic was drowned that day in Berry's Bay. It was an awful bad day and night for the seafaring people. The good Lord was looking after me or I would have been drowned also.

When I left Atlantic, I wanted to take my oldest daughter Ethel Marie with me to spend awhile with her Grandmother Sidney, but Thelma did not want her to go. It was good that she was not with me. A small child of six would have been scared to death or might have been drowned.

I have been from Atlantic to Portsmouth Island many times since the storm. Sometimes it can get mighty rough on the water, especially when you cross the mouth of the Pamlico Sound, but I will never forget the night of August 9, 1924.

# Portsmouth Island People

The people that were natives of Portsmouth were honest, decent, hardworking people. The men were seafaring and were either in the lifesaving service on the island, or were fishermen. Some of the men worked as hunting guides in the winter. When I speak of fishermen, I mean they fished, oystered and clamed for a living. They worked hard, but always managed to make a fairly good living for themselves and their families. They owned their own homes and boats.

When they came in from fishing, they always gathered around to mend their nets. On days it was too bad to go fishing, they would sit in their fish house for hours and mend nets. I enjoyed these days, as a young boy. It was enjoyable helping and listening to the older men tell tales of things that happened on Portsmouth long before I was born.

Winter was the time to hunt and oyster. You could catch oysters during the months that had an "R" in them. That is, September, October, November, December, January, February, March and April. In the summer, they fished and clammed, some would catch crabs. The women stayed at home and took care of the children and they kept their homes spotlessly clean. They also took pride in keeping everything in their yards as clean as could be. Their children were clean and neat even though there might be a patch or two on their pants or dresses. The mothers taught the girls to read, write, and sew. The boys were taught to read, write, and keep their rooms neat.

The children were sent to school when they were old enough. Most of them could say their ABC's and print their names before they started to school. If the year was not stormy, school lasted six months. If it was stormy, the teachers were afraid to go in the school. I remember one year that we had school only two months. A storm came in October and scared the teacher so bad that she left the island and didn't return.

*The Island School was off the straight road.* (Photo courtesy of Frances Eubanks)

The women sewed for themselves, their husbands, and their children. Everyone wore homemade clothes. In later years, people ordered clothing for parties and church from catalogues. They made lace, and ruffle trimming to go on their dresses by crocheting and tatting. Sometimes you could go by a house and see the ladies sitting around all working with their fingers making fancy work to go on the baby dresses or little girl's dresses. Five or six ladies would sometimes gather in one living room to sew and visit at the same time. They made quilts, blankets, pillows, and feather beds. The pillows and feather beds were made from the feathers of the fowl that the men killed in winter. They used thick cloth called "bed ticking" and stuffed with feathers. Every family had these to sleep on, they were real warm in the winter.

The island children played together. The small ones would play where their moms could watch them, and the ones big enough played outside, but were also expected to help their mother. The ladies always took time to show the girls how to do work. People in those days took the time to teach their children how to keep house and do the necessary things that had to be done. They would read the Bible to them and teach them how to live and love each other and God. How I wish things were more like that today.

The people on Portsmouth had pretty gardens. They started planting in early spring so they could have fresh vegetables as soon as possible. Most every family raised potatoes, tomatoes, corn, cabbage, cucumbers, squash, beans, peas, watermelons, and the prettiest collards. As a boy, I saw all of these things growing on Portsmouth Island.

They have always been dew berries on the island during the months of May and June. People still go there to pick berries to make pies and jelly. There used to be the largest fig trees and two or three in every yard. Women made fig preserves enough to last all year. Fig preserves and hot biscuits are good on cold mornings for breakfast.

The people were mostly soft spoken, never seeming to get nervous and excited as people of today. They lived together helping each other the best they could. There were two or three ladies that were mid wives. They took care of the ladies when children were born. There were no doctors on the island after the Marine hospital closed. When somebody got real sick, they went to the mainland by boat.

For past time, the people gathered after supper at one house and the best reader would read aloud to the group. Many people went often to my Aunt Melissa's home. She was a good reader, sometimes she would read for two or three hours. After Thelma and I were married, they would gather to mamas and papas and Thelma would read to the group. They would stay until bedtime, then take their lanterns and go home. Most of the time, the stories would be continued until the next night. This went on until the book was read.

Christmas, New Years, other holidays and Saturday nights the older people and teenagers would gather at the old Marine hospital and had square dances. After the hospital was destroyed, they gathered in living rooms to dance. Uncle SamTolson was a great dancer as was Uncle Dave Salter. The people would come from Cedar Island to dance, everyone would have a good time. The people that came from Cedar Island would spend the night at a friend's house. Sometimes the men would play checkers or other games to amuse themselves.

# The Pigott Family

Aunt Rosa Abbott, her brothers Joe and Henry, and her sisters Dorcas and Ann, were among the African Americans to live on Portsmouth Island. There had been other people of color on the island from time to time, but this family stayed and made the island their home. It was known that Aunt Rosa was a descendant of slaves from before the Civil War. She was a midwife and also acted as a doctor and a nurse. She helped all the people in every way she could. Everyone loved her very much.

*Thelma Styron Salter, Dot Salter Willis, and Lizzie Pigott spent an afternoon chatting on the front porch.* (Photo courtesy of Dot S. Willis private collection.)

No one remembered her husband, but she had children. She and her daughter, Leah, worked in a gristmill that was on the island. They also fished and oystered for a living – just like a man. Aunt Rosa was roasting oysters one day down on Doctors Creek. Her clothes caught on fire and she soon died because she was burned so badly.

Leah, had the last name of Pigott. She had three sons, Ike, Ed, and Henry. Her four daughters were Mattie, Georgia, Rachel, and Elizabeth, who was called "Lizzie". Henry and Lizzie remained on the island and were my life-long friends. They were decent honest folk. Many days we worked side by side oystering or fishing. I don't remember their father. They never talked about him, nor did they mention who he was or where he was. We never asked. We loved them because they were nice folks.

Henry was not dark in color, he was like an Indian in appearance. He talked like all of the people on the Outer Banks- with an old English brogue. He told me stories about his life and things he could remember that happened on the island.

We never heard about a color barrier in those days. There was no need; we were all in the work together. The Pigotts attended the Methodist Church that we did. They visited with us and lived among us. Henry was just a little older than me, so we grew up together. I always go back to see Henry when I go to Portsmouth, a finer man I never knew.

Lizzie helped Henry oyster and fish. My wife took our two oldest children "down the banks" to Lizzie's house to get their hair cut. They always enjoyed going there.

Henry and Lizzie's sister, Rachel, left the island to find work. She secured a job in the Naval Air Base in Newport News, Virginia. She worked there until she retired. She then returned to Portsmouth to live with Henry and Lizzie. She only drew two checks before she died from a heart attack. She is buried in the Community Cemetery on the island she loved so. In later years after Lizzie had a stroke, Henry took care of her. She was disabled for quite awhile before she died. Neither Henry nor Lizzie ever married. They worked hard and took care of each other. After Lizzie died, Henry was never the same. He was lonesome for his sister. Lizzie was buried in the Babb Cemetery behind Mrs. Lillian Babb's home.

Henry was living when I started to write this book. He fished for a living, but in later years, he picked up the mail from the mail boat when she went by the island on her way to Ocracoke. He poled out in a small skiff to get the mail. He also picked up passengers and usually gave the captain a grocery list for the people on the island. Merchants at Ocracoke filled the orders and sent them back by someone coming our way or by the mail boat the next day. The grocery stores were all gone from the island at this time.

Eventually, Henry became ill and went to stay with a family at Ocracoke. It was a sad day when he died. The obituary in the newspaper read as follows:

*Henry Pigott in his backyard. (Photo courtesy of Dot S. Willis private collection.)*

*Henry Pigott, 74, the last permanent male resident on Portsmouth Island, died Tuesday in the Albemarle General Hospital, Elizabeth City, N. C. The funeral service was conducted at 10 a.m. Thursday in the Methodist Church on Portsmouth. Mr. Pigott was buried in the cemetery plot at the rear of the Babb home near the church.*

*Officiating were the Rev. Carroll Beale, Pastor of the Ocracoke Methodist Church and the Rev. John Barrow of the Assembly of God.*

*Mr. Pigott was considered the patriarch of the island. He had been in declining health for the past year. Mr. Pigott, who was born on Portsmouth, leaves no immediate survivors. His sister, Elizabeth, died on the island in 1960 and is buried in the same cemetery as her brother.*

A bronze plaque hangs in the church on the island in memory of Henry Pigott.

# Jodie Styron

Mr. Jodie Styron, native of Portsmouth Island, N. C. Born on April 12, 1873 in the Marine hospital. At the time of his birth, there were about six hundred people living on the island. During the Civil War, around 1860, the three-hundred bed hospital had eighteen doctors and many nurses and orderlies. Quite a few babies were born there, I was fortunate to know Mr. Jodie and have him for a life-long friend.

After the Civil War ended, some years later, the hospital was turned into a telegraph office and an apartment house. The first money Mr. Jodie ever made was when he was a small boy cleaning the canteens for the operator of the office. He gave Mr. Jodie fifty cents. He was ten years old.

On November 23, 1899, he married Miss Annie Bragg. They lived together on the island for fifty-seven years. They had happy times as well as sad days in all of those years. They never had children. Miss Annie's brother, Mr. Tom Bragg, lived with them. Together they operated a gun club. Mr. Tom and Mr. Jodie were good guides. Mr. Tom was well known for his marksmanship and his imitation of the Canada wild goose.

Mrs. Annie died on June 12, 1956. Shortly after her death, Mr. Jodie went to live in Atlantic with Mr. Miand Willis, also a native of Portsmouth Island. He lived with him for quite some time, then moved in with Mr. Walt Nelson and his family. As he grew older, he became helpless and was confined to the house. I used to go by and see him. He would talk about the old days and the years he spent on Portsmouth. He loved to tell of the days long gone by and the time that he spent with Mrs. Annie and their friends. I think that he always wished he could have spent his last days on the island.

One day, he became ill and was taken to the Sea Level Hospital. He died on April 3, 1964. He was 91 years old.

# "Uncle" Samuel C. Tolson

Mr. Sam Tolson was born on Portsmouth Island on November 7, 1840. He lived, died, and was buried on the island. When he died on November 17, 1930, his stay on the island had llasted over 90 years.

He was a nice old man when I was a boy. He told me many interesting stories of days on Portsmouth when he was a boy. Once he said the ducks, geese, and brandt were so thick that he could stick a bush down on the banks of the shore and kill all he could carry home.

He remembered when people had no window panes in their homes and had no matches to make fires. They did as the Indians did. They rubbed sticks together to start a fire. They had wooden shutters at the windows to close against the wind, rain, and cold. He told me that when he was a boy, there was a big fort on Beacon Island, a big castle on Castle Rock, and folks were living on a large rock known as Flounder Slew Rock.

Sam smoked a clay pipe with a long stem. When he dressed up, he wore a

*Uncle Sam Tolson* (*Photo courtesy of Dot S. Willis private collection.*)

derby hat and a stiff-breasted shirt with gold studs in it. He was rather sharp looking for that day.

He traveled a little up and down the coast by boat. Once he was in Elizabeth City in 1865. He was arrested and accused of assassinating President Abraham Lincoln. He matched the description of John Wilkes Booth. He wore the same size hat, shoes, and was the same size in statue. It took folks on Portsmouth a long time to convince the officers that Uncle Sam was not Booth. Sam never went to Elizabeth City again.

# Fred Cannon

Fred was born on February 5, 1916 in South River. His parents were Louis and Sina Cannon.

In 1964, Fred came to Atlantic to spend time with my brother Ross and his wife Gladys. He stayed to work with my brother and after awhile they decided to go to Portsmouth to go fishing and fish crab pots. Ross had a boat with a small cabin on her. There was just enough room for one man to sleep, so Fred took a small tent to sleep in. They planned to spend a week or two. After a short while, they decided to go back to Atlantic and get supplies and then go back to Portsmouth to spend the winter. Fred said that it was a hard winter. One night he woke up and it was snowing on him and on Ross. They both worked hard, long hours. They decided to build a camp to stay in, so they could cook and sleep inside.

They gathered driftwood, boards that washed up on the beach and from abandoned houses to build this camp. After work, they would go around the shore in a small skiff down the banks to see the few people that were living on the island at that time. Miss Elma Dixon, Marian Gray Babb, and Henry Pigott were there. Mrs. Jean Burke would come over from Ocracoke to stay at her home on Portsmouth. Fred loved to go down there and talk with these folks about days long ago and how the people lived on the island. They enjoyed seeing Ross and Fred.

Mrs. Burke hired Fred to cut grass and he became her caretaker. Fred helped all the people. He helped Henry cut the grass around his home. Then they'd mow around the paths, around the post office, and around the church.

Fred was what some people call a "loner." He loved Portsmouth, so when Ross returned home to Atlantic, Fred remained on the island. He called Portsmouth his adopted home.

Everyone who knew Fred liked him, he never met a stranger. He made friends easily, yet he loved to live alone, fishing his crab pots and keeping the grass cut and doing odd jobs for all of the people on the island.

# A Dog Named Key

When the ship *Messenger of Peace* came ashore off Portsmouth in 1922, she had on board the prettiest black dog. He was a large dog and was black all over, except for a patch of white on his throat and chest. When Captain Coleman left the island, he could not carry the dog with him, so he gave him to my father, John Wallace Salter. We were told that the Messenger of Peace was on her way to the Florida Keys. That's why papa named the dog Key.

Papa loved the dog , as did all the rest of the family. Key was well behaved, he had lots of sense and could learn easily. He became quiet a hunter. Papa would carry Key with him when he went bird hunting. He would go get the birds that fell on land or in the water. Papa said, "Key brings back birds that I did not know I killed."

Key liked to go hunting with my brother Charlie. Charlie liked to hunt for minks, there were a lot of minks on the island. Key and Charlie had many good hunts together as they both enjoyed long walks. They always brought back a mink or two. Charlie would skin them and sell the hides.

When papa went out in his skiff, you could always see Key sitting on the bow. He was a good companion for papa.

One day, one of the boys had been away on a trip. Key was getting old, but he ran to meet him. Key was so big he could put his paws on a man's shoulders, he jumped up and as he did, he broke a blood vessel. He bled to death because we did not have a veterinarian on the island. It was too far away to carry him to one. Key was buried close by our house. We missed him and were all sorry that he had died.

I can never remember us having another dog while we lived on Portsmouth island.

# John Wallace "Governor: of Shell Castle

Captain John Wallace later known as "Governor" Wallace lived on a large rock island near Portsmouth. The island was named Castle Rock. Wallace built a large house there that he called Shell Castle. He installed a beacon light there in 1798.

This island was made of rock and shells that were dumped there by the ships that came into the Portsmouth Inlet (Ocracoke Inlet). John Wallace was born in England, but he came to Portsmouth as a young man. He lived there until he went into business and operated wharfs for ships and built his "castle" on Castle Rock.

"Governor" Wallace was buried on Portsmouth in 1810. He is buried in the Wallace private cemetery on the end of the island known as the Sheep Island. It is located close to the place where my home was when I lived on the Island.

The epitaph on Governor Wallace's grave is written in old English and reads as follows:

Here is deposited the remains of Captain John Wallace Governor of Shell Castle, who departed this life July 22, 1810. Age 52 years and 6 months.

*Shell Castle Mournes; Your price is in the dust; Your boast, your glory in the dreary grave, Your sun is set ne'er to illume again. This sweet asylum from this At- lantic wave. He's here be- neath this monumental*

*tomb. Thy awful gloom amid the silent dead. Thy founder lies whose sainted soul we trust to heaven. His mansion has its journey sped. Mourn, Charity benevolence be wail. With one hospitality his lots deplore. His own with one unanimous acclaim. Misfortunes Son will view his like no more.*

Other graves in the Wallace Cemetery are:

---

**In Memory of Mrs. Rebecca Wallace Wife of John Wallace**
Born 11th June 1771
Departed this life 22nd November 1823
*She left this world with shining hope for a better one Leaving three daughters and two sons, bereaved by her death.*

---

Two small headstones made together:

| **Sara J. Babb** | **Virginia S. Babb** |
|---|---|
| Born Sept. 28, 1896 | Born Dec. 16, 1906 |
| Died Oct. 6, 1896 | Died Jan. 30, 1907 |

---

**Son of Millard & Rebecca Mayo**
**ELEAZAR**
Born April 3, 1827 • Died June 17, 1858

*Reflect and see as you pass by as you are now so once was I as I am now so soon you'll be prepared for death and follow me.*

Elizabeth Mayo is also buried in the Wallace Cemetery.

*Ed. note: The island known as Shell Castle was in the Ocracoke Inlet. It was also known as Shell Island and Castle Rock. It is no longer visible.)*

# My Friend Jesse McWilliams

Mr. Charlie and Mrs. Annie McWilliams moved their family to Portsmouth Island from Ocracoke. Mr. Charlie had been stationed at the Hatteras life-saving station. He was put in command at the station at Portsmouth Island.

They had six boys and two girls. The boys were Milton, Jesse, John, Murry, Robert, and Clarence. The girls were Eliza and Margaret. They were all nice children, a nice family and well loved by the people on the island.

Mr. Charlie was the first man to put a sand fence along the beach, to help hold the sand so the beach would build up. He helped in many ways to protect the island and the people. Mrs. Annie was a fine woman always ready to help her neighbors in time of trouble and was like a second mother to me.

I loved all the family very much, but Jesse and I were closer than all the rest. I was a few years older than he, but we always played together when we were small. Jesse was about four years old when his family moved to Portsmouth. I was about seven and Jesse was four when he moved to Portsmouth. When Jesse was old enough, we went to school together, played and stayed together most of the time. He spent the night with me sometime and then I spent the night with him. He has been my lifelong friend and I love him as a brother.

As we grew older, we went to parties, dances, and sometimes to church together. We visited the old people and the shut-ins. We enjoyed sitting with the old folks and listening to the stories they would tell us about the island before we could remember. Jesse and I had a friend named Ed Dixon that went with us lots of times. Jesse, Ed, and I were true friends and are to this very day. Jesse lives in Norfolk, Virginia, and Ed lives on Harker's Island, North Carolina.

One night, Ed, Jesse, and I decided we would go see an old lady we called Aunt Mandy Jane. We stayed awhile with her as we loved to hear her talk. We would tease her and she would get mad at us, but that would soon be over. She would run us home, before long we would go back to see her. Aunt Mandy Jane had cats. She loved them and they were always around her house. One night when she was mad at us, we caught her big white cat and climbed up on the roof of her house and dropped him down the chimney right at her feet. She ran out of the house screaming at us because she knew we did it. We were bad boys, but we were just trying to have a little fun, never meaning to hurt anyone.

After leaving Aunt Mandy Jane's another night, we had been drinking some strong drink. We could always manage to get some, even on Portsmouth Island. Jesse and I decided we would make a little trip to see Joe Abbott. When we got there, Joe said, "Come in boys, I am so glad you have come to see me."

We got Joe to play the organ for us. He loved to play and sing and he sang "Dear wife, I have found the model Church and worshipped there today. It made me think of the good old days before my hair was gray. We talked and laughed with Joe for awhile, then we went on our way.

We took a few more drinks, then we decided we would stop by to see Uncle Sam Tolson. Now, he had been sick for some time. We went up to the house and he told us to come in. he said, "boys, I am down in my back, but I am so glad you stopped to see me." We sat down and began to talk to him and listen to him tell of days gone by. We asked Uncle Same if he didn't think a drink might help him feel better. He said that he guessed so. So, we gave him a good big drink and he was soon sitting on the side of his bed. We talked on for about an hour and soon he said, "Boys, I think another little drink will help me." So, we gave him another big drink. Now, it wasn't long before Uncle Sam was feeling real good.

We decided if we had a prayer meeting with Uncle Sam he would get well. We all knelt down to pray. Jesse led in prayer and I got to laughing so much I could not pray. Uncle Sam was still praying when we left his house. It was getting late, so we had to make our way home in the dark. We got there and managed to get in the house without waking mama and papa.

When I sit and think of some of the things we did as boys, I can't help but laugh. Some things are not so funny as they were when we were growing up.

Jesse and I shared many happy days together on Portsmouth island. We go back together from time to time, We are planning a trip in the near future, hope we live long enough to make it one more time.

*The cooling house was the islanders original means of refrigation. The little house was constructed to catch the prevailing winds. A pan of water was placed inside with the food. The sea breeze would blow across the water bringing down the temperature within helping to preserve food.*

# The Old Man Who Told Tales

When my brothers and I were small, there was an old man who lived on Portsmouth Island, the end that we lived on. He always tattled and told tales on the boys, seeming to enjoy seeing us boys get whippings from our mamas and papas.

Of course, we were always doing things that we should not do, there being no movies of television on the island. We had to find things to amuse ourselves. We turned over people's small skiffs, climbed trees, waded ditches, swam the creeks, ran horses and cattle and did numerous other things for fun.

This old man would come to see mama and papa, but before he left, he would always tell something that would get us in "hot water."

One day, my brother Tom and I saw him coming to our house. Papa was not at home, but mama was at home ironing. She stopped long enough to go to the door and call papa. He was over to Uncle Dave's house, so we knew right away that the man had something to tell papa. He had come for the purpose of telling another tale on us. We wondered what it was this time.

Now, we had a cross bow, as many boys did in those days. It would shoot straight and strong. It was strong enough to kill birds and even people if you hit them just right. We decided that this was the time to stop the old man from telling any tales on us and the other boys on the island. My brother Tom and I looked for a piece of steel or some hard object to shoot in our cross bow. Mama had discarded an old iron cook stove. It was out in the back yard, so we broke off a piece of the stove and it came off nice and sharp. We put it in the cross bow and started toward the house. Brother Tom said, "Ben, where are you going to shoot him?"

I said, "In the head."

Tom said, "My goodness, don't do that, you'll kill him."

So, I decided to shoot elsewhere. Tom opened the back door real easy. I could see where the old man was sitting while waiting for papa to come home. I stuck the bow inside the door just as quiet as I could. He always wore high top boots or shoes. The ones he had on that day were laced up in front, almost to his knees. I aimed for the leg and hit him just above the ankle bone. He jumped up and the fell down on the floor and hollered as loud as he could. He thought that he was killed.

It scared my mama almost to death. She ran out of the house calling for papa, saying, "John, come quick, they have killed him. Please, come quick!" She knew that it was us and what we had done.

Papa came running. When he saw what had happened, he gave us the worst whipping, but that old man never came to our house to tell tales on us again. He had a sore leg for a long time.

# The Sick Man on A Boat

One day a boat owned by a man from Atlantic came close up to our landing and anchored. That night it turned awful cold and the creek froze over. It froze so hard and thick that a man could walk on the ice. The boat was frozen in. Now, the man in the boat was sick. We found this out when someone walked out to see him.

My mother heard about this and being that she was a kind woman, wanted to do something for the man. She made a big pot of brandt soup. She called my brother Tom and me to carry a bowl of the soup out to the man in the boat.

We started out with the soup, walking on the ice. Mama told us to be careful and not spill it as it was very hot and would burn us. She thought that, it would make the old man feel better if he could eat. When we got there, the door to the cabin was fastened. We knocked and told him we had some soup. He was quite sick but managed to get up and open the door.

We went inside, gave him the soup and sat down to talk to him awhile. Soon we told him we must go back home so mama would not be worried about us. When we got outside, we decided to have some fun-or so we thought. We found a real big thick piece of ice. It was big enough to do the work. So, just as quiet as a mouse I climbed up on the side of the boat and up on the cabin. I had to be careful because my hands were almost frozen from carrying the piece of ice. I placed this on top of the old man's stove pipe that came out of the top of the cabin, and just as quietly, I climbed down. Brother Tom and I hid in the bushes on the shore side to watch.

Soon the old man came out with smoke after him. He just boiled out of his cabin. He was coughing and choking. He could hardly get his breath. Of course, this tickled us almost to death. We thought it was funny, but our sins found us out.

The old man got well and managed to come to our house to thank mama for the soup. But before he left, he told papa what had happened that day. Boy! We got a whipping that I have never forgotten until this day.

My papa said, "Some day you boys will be old and you too might get sick and need help. What if someone did the same to you?" We hung our heads in shame. We just thought we were having fun. Now, we are both old, but we never played any more pranks on sick  people.

# Cottage Lighthouses

Cottages on the briny deep were an actuality for many years up and down the coast around Portsmouth. They were little white cottages with green shutters and ruffled curtains at the windows. Once there were eight of these little houses up and down Pamlico Sound. Their lights and bells marked the dangerous reefs and shoals. Gradually, they were abandoned as the Coast Guard's channel lighting system was improved. For more than forty years, they have been just memories in the minds of those that knew and saw them. Some people have a few pictures of these little cottages.

Mr. Kelly Robinson of Atlantic, formally of Portsmouth Island, can remember them well as he spent a part of his childhood aboard the one at Southwest Point, near his home on Portsmouth. There were others located at Pamlico Point, Brandt Island, Oliver's Reef, Harbor Island, Northwest Point, Gull Shoal, and Hatteras. They were all very much alike. The only one that was different was Northwest Point that was octagon shaped.

The cottages were boarded by means of iron ladders set down the side of the framework from the porch to the water line. According to Kelly, they were comfortable, well equipped, and spotlessly clean, very roomy and had every convenience available in those days.

The cottages were built on large iron standards, more than two feet in diameter set in a concrete base. A fifth standard ran through the center of the cottage to its tower where the great brass lamps were located.

"Those lights were the prettiest," recalled Kelly. "They were beautiful at night with each of the eight prisms reflecting a rainbow of colors, the brass shining, and the light flashing from the eight windows."

He helped to clean the lamps, trim the wicks, polish the brass, and fill them with kerosene. Two lamps were used each night. One was lit at sunset and it lasted until midnight when it was replaced by a second one that burned till dawn. Each day these and extra ones for emergency were carefully cleaned and tended.

About 1900, Mr. Charlie Keeler was caught in a violent storm while returning from a trip to New Bern. He made shore at Portsmouth and was taken into the home of Mrs. Roberts and was cared for by her and her daughter. However, in spite of their efforts, he died the next day of exposure. Miss Annie, his wife, then moved into their house ashore and Mr. Ed Keeler replaced his brother at Southwest Point. A new keeper occupied the octagonal house at Northwest Point for several years, but the great August storm of 1903 caused it to be abandoned. The sturdy little white pine structure withstood the force of the storm, but it had outlived its usefulness.

Another time, Kelly Robinson remembered, "One time, Mrs. Keeler brought down a servant from Bridgeport. Her name was Mrs. McLane. She was a stout lady. I remember that she used to sing a great deal. Her favorite song was *Safe in the Lifeboat, Sailor Pull for the Shore.*"

Most of the supplies were brought from the mainland by a sidewheeler paddle boat named, *The Violet.* She also brought the inspectors for their regular visits.

The lights at Southwest and Northwest Points, five miles out in the sound and five miles apart, were tended by two brothers from Bridgeport, Connecticut. Mr. Ed and Mr. Charlie Keeler. Each maintained a household aboard their respective lighthouses. They also shared a large home ashore on Portsmouth Island, known as the Keeler Place, which although over a hundred years old, is still partially standing.

*Kelly Robinson (Mary Elizabeth Mason's private collection)*

Mr. Charlie and his wife Miss Annie lived in the house at Southwest Point, and for a number of years little Kelly Robinson lived with them.  His mother did the laundry and his uncle, James Willis ran the relief boat which carried supplies out from the island.

"They had the best of everything," said Kelly Robinson. "Downstairs there was the big living room where Miss Annie kept her high topped pump organ." Kelly learned to play the organ. He described the rest of the home with a first floor with a big bedroom, a combination living and dining room, a kitchen with a coal and wood range, plenty of closets and supply rooms. Rainwater for drinking and other household uses was caught in big tanks from which ran pipes to carry the water to the spigots in the kitchen.

Life there was comfortable and fascinating to little Kelly. He slept in one of the two bedrooms on the second floor. He fished from his porch, and spent hours watching the variety of marine life in the water. He helped Miss Annie with the household chores.

The most fascinating of all was the big light on the top of the house with its little walkway and a lightning rod on its roof. The great brass lamps were cleaned, polished, trimmed, and stored in a special room on the second floor. From here an iron ladder led up to the light tower.

Mr. Ed was sickly for a number of years. This particular day we sighted the *Violet* coming and we thought that the inspector would be aboard. Mr. Ed was resting, he got up, put on his uniform and his cap with the big brass lighthouse on the front. The weather was rough and Mr. Ed wasn't well enough to be up and about. "I'll tie her up, Mr. Ed, "I said.

"No, son, "he replied, "You're too little to handle her." Ten-year-old Kelly climbed down around the center standard and out onto the iron framework underneath. He caught the hauser from the *Violet* and made her fast with two half hitches. At the captain's orders, he stood clear in case his knot didn't hold. He'd forgotten to give it a clinching hitch, but she held just the same. He was proud as the captain climbed up and congratulated him.

Mr. Ed died when Kelly was twelve. "I was sleeping upstairs. Mr. Ed had lain down on the sofa in the big living room about dawn. He had just taken off his shoes and socks, when Miss Dinah called me. I ran downstairs, and there was Mr. Ed – dead. I started to get dressed, but in my excitement, I put on his socks instead of mind. They were still warm. You can bet that I got them off in a hurry!"

Kelly ran upstairs, put out a light, and flew the flag at half mast – union down- a distress signal. This was seen by fishermen aboard their boats off-shore and they came to the rescue.

The cottage at Hatteras was manned by Mr. Angel who had come down from the north. One day his daughter fell through the trapdoor in the cottage and was drowned. Then the Angels adopted a Negro boy named Tom. After their deaths, he spent his life in their big stone house at Hatteras where he took in boarders and ran an ice cream business.

As the cottages were replaced by modern channel lights, each was abandoned and torn down and dumped into the water below to be claimed as wreckage by finders. It bothered Mr. Kelly that because of government regulations, such fine little houses had to come to such a sad end. After this, Kelly worked at the Pilentary Clubhouse (a private hunting club) about ten miles from Portsmouth.

This story was told by Kelly Robinson, my life long friend. He stayed a part of his last days at my home in Atlantic and we sat for hours and talked about Portsmouth Island. Kelly's foster son, Monroe Mason, is my son-in-law. Kelly was loved by many people. He was custodian of the Atlantic School for many years. The school yearbook was dedicated to him in 1957.

His obituary appeared in the *Carteret News Times.*
William Kelly Robinson, 79, Atlantic, N. C., died Friday at the Sea Level Hospital.

Mr. Robinson's funeral service was held at 2 p.m., Sunday at the United Methodist Church, with Rev. Bobby Smith, Pastor and the Rev. John Spencer, officiating. Burial was in the Atlantic community Cemetery.

He is survived by a foster son, William Monroe Mason, one half sister, Mrs. Bessie Scott, and four grandchildren by his foster son. Uncle Kelly Robinson is mourned by all that knew and loved him.

# The Pilentary Club House

The Pilentary clubhouse was about ten miles up the beach from Portsmouth. It was owned and operated as a hunting lodge for many years by a man named Rodgers. He sold it to Mr. Jordan L. Mont. The keeper of the clubhouse was Mr. Alvin T. Mason. He and his family lived there year around.

He and his wife Mrs. Amelia, "Miss Mellie", we called her, had a large family of sixteen children. These children were raised for a time on the outer banks at the clubhouse. Mr. Alvin hired a teacher to come over. I remember one, her name was Rosa Felton.

The cook was a colored man, he was a descendent of the slaves of the Civil War period. He was a strong man even though he dressed as a woman at times. He always wore a nice clean apron and dipped snuff like the women did. He could play the organ. One day, a friend of mine, Jesse McWilliams, and I walked up the beach to the Pilentary Club and he played the organ for us. One song that he played and sang was "Dear Wife, I Found the Model Church and Worshipped There Today." He lived on Portsmouth for a while and played this same song for us.

Kelly Robinson helped in the kitchen and the dining room. He worked there until the club was washed away in the big storm of 1933. Kelly and the colored man would take the laundry and walk all the way to Portsmouth to do the washing.

After Mr. Alvin moved with his family and Kelly to Atlantic, Mr. Roby Fulcher and Mrs. Adeline took care of the club for about two years. Then Mr. John Salter and his wife Ina Mason Salter took care of the clubhouse. Their two boys were small when the clubhouse washed away. One day, a bad storm came and washed away all of the camps and houses on the beach. The Pilentary Clubhouse was one of them.

The night was a long one for the Salter family as they had to take refuge on a big sand hill on the beach thinking all the night they would be washed into the sea or sound and be drowned.

The little boys were so afraid, their Aunt Polly was with them. One of the boys looked at her and said, "Aunt Polly, the crabs will pick our heads before morning." He was afraid they were going to be drowned. They were saved and moved to Atlantic. Today, there is only a barren sandy strip of beach where once this big clubhouse stood.

*(Ed. note: The Pilentary Club washed away in the hurricane of 1933. Many houses on Portsmouth were damaged and some were demolished. After the storm, some families left Portsmouth and moved to the mainland.)*

# The Church on the Island

The deed for the church property was recorded July 2, 1840, but it was drawn on March 7, 1840. It was deeded by Samuel and Susan D. Dudley to the trustees of the Methodist Episcopal Church. The trustees were Samuel Dudley, Wallas Whitehurst, William Dixon, Wallis Styron, and Thomas W. Styron. The witnesses were John Mayo and George Dill. The deed was recorded by David Rumley, Clerk of Court in Beaufort, North Carolina.

The first church was a two-story building that measured 36 by 30 feet. The old building was destroyed in a storm in 1899. As we see it today, the church was rebuilt by the residents of the island with money donated by the people and by the Methodist Conference.

The first church was organized earlier. A church was mentioned in the Conference Journal in 1828. It must have been formed even earlier. At that time, the presiding elder was Joseph Carson. The pastors were Irvin Atkinson and Alfred Norman. John Kerr served in 1829. Others included: Raymond R. Minor in 1830, Thompson Garrard from 1831 through 1832, Benjamin N. Barnes in 1833, Thomas Garrard in 1834, Henry Wood 1835, James M. Darden 1836, William M. Jordon in 1837, Junius W. Jackson in 1838, WW. Turner in 1839, W. M. Walsh in 1840, John R. McIntosh in 1841, J. B. Corn in 1842, N. A. Hooker in 1843, W. S. Chaffin in 1844, R. A. Claughton in 1845, Charles Parker in 1846, Bird S. Turner in 1847. Between 1848 and 1851 various ministers were supplied by the Conference. J. M. Sharpe arrived in 1851 and James J. Hines in 1852, Alexander Gattis in 1853.

In 1854, the church was turned over to the Washington Charge and W. H. Wheeler served as the pastor until 1860. At some point, the island was occupied by federal troops and the minister's post was vacated. However, there is mention of A. R. Raven in 1861 and 1862, and C. P. Jones in 1863.

George E. Wyche was listed as the minister in 1867 and a supply pastor in1868 and 1869.

In 1896, Rev. R. L. Warlick arrived to fill his new appointment. He preached Saturday night January 25th for the first time. He went home with James Mayo to spend the night and seemed to be in good health and good spirits when he went to bed. When he was called for breakfast, there was no response. Brother Mayo entered the room and found that the pastor had answered a "higher calling."

At home, Reverend Warlick's wife was praying for her husband's success in delivering his sermon. She was stricken with the startling declaration, "Brother Warlick is not here, for God has taken him."

Reverend R. F. Taylor did not arrive to serve until December of that year. S. T. Mayle arrived in 1898 and B. C. Humble served in 1899, until August, when one of the worst storms ever remembered hit the island and the church was destroyed, along with many homes.

The people of Portsmouth were much concerned over not having a church where they could go and worship. Many gave of their money and time along with the help of the Methodist Conference and built the church that is standing today. The beautiful little church has stood as a "light upon a hill." Reverend Benson H. Black was the first pastor for the new church and served from 1900 until 1904. It was then taken over by the New Bern Charge who supplied E. W. Read. Preachers by the name of Watson, Boone, Daniels, Webster, Pittman, Eure, Ipock and Hocutt preached until 1916.

While Reverend W. Hoyle, Jr. was there my oldest sister, Pearl and Jerome Fulcher were married on September 30, 1917. Pearl and her husband were well-known. She had been voted as the prettiest girl in Carteret County. Jerome was a World War I veteran. People came from Davis, Atlantic, Ocracoke,

*Pearl Fulcher, voted Prettiest Girl in Carteret County*

and Hatteras. The witnesses were Mary Sneed, Catherine Sneed, and Dave Salter. They later moved and built a home in New Bern.

The church had many preachers after this. In 1918, Guy Hamilton arrived and M. B. Cox was there in 1919.

November 8-10 1939, the final session of the North Carolina Conference of the Methodist Episcopal Church South met and dissolved the church. This permitted the North Carolina Conference of the Methodist Church to come into being. In 1839, W. H. Brady was sent to serve both Portsmouth and Ocrakcoke. William R. Dixon arrived in 1941 and stayed until 1945. N. M. McDonald, a retired minister arrived in 1945 and was there in 1946. Charles J. Tilley supplied in 1947, however there is no mention of the church after this time. By that time, only a few people were living on the island. Although many preachers held services on the island, there is not record. I known that Reverend Richard Shinkle preached at the church many times while he was serving in Ocracoke. He told me that he baptized Henry Pigott. He indicated that Henry had also been baptized many years before, as his name was on the church roll.

Mrs. Mattie Gilgo donated the organ to the church. Her husband served in the life-saving service and she and her husband and children were active members. Her husband died while still a young man and left her a widow with four small children. They grew up on the island and always attended the church.

In 1938, the roll of officers for the church were Ethel Gilgo superintendent; Lillian Babb, assistant superintendent, Marion G. Babb, secretary; and Elma Dixon, treasurer. Members of class one were Ethel Gilgo, Jesse Lee Babb, Wilford A. Dixon, Lionel Gilgo, Jr., Estelle Roberts, and Elton Roberts. Members of class two were Cecil Gilgo, Dorothy M. Salter, some of these people have passed away since I started this book and all of them have moved from the island. However the people were active in the little church and still love to go back there from time to time.

The Bible in the church was published in 1887. Miss Marian G. Babb and Miss Elma Dixon still deep the church very clean and neat for the many visitors who come from time to time. There is a collection plate for contributions. The money goes for the upkeep of the church, such as pain and shingles. My family always goes to the church when they go back to Portsmouth. Sometimes we read from God's book and pray, sing a song and go out thanking God that we have been blessed to visit this church and this island once more.

On Saturday July 6, 1968, Doctor Ted Best and Anne Haley Vipperman were married in the church. This was the first wedding since 1917. People arrived by boats, airplanes and beach buggies. A couple on Ocracoke heard there was to be a wedding in the little white church and came by sailing schooner. It was an exciting time for the couple and they people that knew them. When 100 casually clad guests, along with Dr. Ted Best of Sea Level and his bride arrived on the island it was surely and unusual thing. Mrs. Rex Best, Ted's mother, dressed for the occasion. Mr. Rex Best, the groom's father was confined to a wheel chair and arrived by plane. Folks gathered about 11 a.m. for the 2 o'clock wedding.

Mickey Dawson decorated the church with red anthariums, chrysanthemums and palms flown in from Hawaii. It made a truly beautiful setting. Afterward, an informal reception was held in the yard of Mrs. Lillian Babb's house, next door to the church.

Priscilla Wills O'Domorell of Chevy Chase, Maryland and Kent Watterson Miller, Jr. of Middleburg Virginia were married in the church on Saturday April 25, 1971. I suppose this will be the last wedding held in the church, however I hope not. I sincerely hope and pray that someone in the National Seashore Park will keep this dear little church just as it is today, white and clean with its steeple reaching toward heaven, pointing everyone that comes, to this island and to God.

My greatest hope is that the church and the houses around it will always stay as they are today. It is a lovely place to see.

In the year 1909, names on the church roll included Jodie Styron, Hub Dixon, Mattie Gilgo, Alfred and Helen Dixon, Willie Willis, Charlies and Polly Midgett, Mahelia Willis, Vera Willis (Vera was the organist, treasurer, and Sunday school superintendent), Joe Abbott, Henry and Lizzie Pigott. Later names added were Nora Dixon, Elma Dixon, Lydia Dixon, Harry Dixon, Mable and Annie Salter, and Cecil Gilgo.

At this time, Mattie Gilgo is one of the oldest living natives of Portsmouth Island. Mrs. Josephine Woolard is the oldest native living at this time. She was born December 17, 1876.

# History of the Post Office

The Portsmouth Island Post Office was established on September 3, 1840 and it was closed on April 11, 1959. After that, mail was sent over from Ocracoke by boat.

| Postmasters | Date of Appointment |
| --- | --- |
| John Rumley | September 3, 1840 |
| Samuel W. Chadwick | September 25, 1840 |
| James M. Williams | April 24, 1841 |
| Abner N. Dixon | November 2, 1842 |
| D. R. Roberts | July 20, 1848 |
| Anson C. Gaskill | September 21, 1849 |
| Robert Whitehurst | January 28, 1850 |
| Samuel E. Davis | March 18, 1851 |
| John O. Wallace | October 4, 1852 |
| Hallis Styron (Styren) | July 16, 1853 |
| Sylvester Dixon | December 17, 1853 |
| William S. Styron (Styren) | October 4, 1856 |
| Wilson F. Piver | January 7, 1857 |
| Paul J. Cornell | October 18, 1865 |
| Jeremiah Abbott | November 17, 1865 |
| John Hill | February 27, 1868 |
| Oscar F. Rue | October 22, 1869 |
| Mary L. Abbott | March 19, 1872 |
| Patsy Williams | September 21, 1876 |
| William O. Williams | November 28, 1887 |
| Lena G. Roberts | October 5, 1897 |
| Ellen A. Daly | August 28, 1899 |
| Ellen A. Willis | May 15, 1901 |
| William H. Babb | June 13, 1907 |
| Joe Roberts | March 1, 1919 |
| Annie Salter | April 1, 1926 |
| Dorothy M. Salter | September 30, 1955 |

Annie Salter was my Uncle Theodore Salter's wife. Dorothy Mae was their daughter. She took over at the death of her mother and was postmaster until the post office was closed in 1959.

Dorothy then moved to Morehead City, North Carolina. In 1959, the mail was sent over by boat from Ocracoke three times a week. Soon the mail ceased to be delivered regularly. A man that comes to the island to see about the few people still living there brings the mail as a favor for his friends.

The post office building is still standing with the flag pole still in the yard. It is a small building, weather beaten by many storms. I wish someone would paint it and fly the flag once more.

*(Ed. note: The post office was restored and painted for the Portsmouth Island Reunion of 2002. To celebrate the ocassion, the postmaster from Ocracoke came for the day and posted mail with a Portsmouth watermark.)*

*Theodore Salter's store was also the location of the post office.*
*(Photo courtesy of Dot S. Willis private collection.)*

# The Lifesaving Station

The first crew to man the Portsmouth Island Lifesaving Station was in 1897, the same year it was built. The surfmen, Dennis Mason, Washington Roberts, Augustus D. Mason, James T. Salter, George W. Gilgo, Jesse J. Newton, & Joseph Dixon.

1899: Captain Charles McWilliams, keeper, & the surfmen Joseph Dixon, George W. Gilgo, Dennis Mason, Leonard W. Nelson, Washington Roberts, James T. Salter, and William T. Willis.

1900: F. G. Terrill, keeper, & surfmen Dennis Mason, Washington Roberts, William F. Willis, Daniel Yeomans and William Fulcher.

1901: F.G. Terrill, keeper & surfmen Washington Roberts, William Fulcher, William F. Willis, Daniel Yeomans, Melville Pigott, Joseph W. Fulcher.

1902: F. G. Terrill, keeper & surfmen, Washington Roberts, W. T. Willis, Melville W. Pigott, Joseph W. Fulcher, H. D. Goodwin, and Alfred H. Chadwick.

1903: F. G. Terrill, keeper & surfmen, W. T. Willis, Melville Pigott, Joseph W. Fulcher, H. D. Goodwin, and Alfred H. Chadwick. During this year, Captain Terrill was asked to resign as keeper due to something that happened when the Vera Cruz came ashore.

1904: Charles McWilliams, keeper & surfmen, Washington Roberts, H. D. Goodwin, Melville M. Pigott, Joseph W. Fulcher, Alfred H. Chadwick, and Herbert S. Pigott.

1905: Charles McWilliams, keeper & surfmen, Washington Roberts, Matthew P. Guthrie, Melville M. Pigott, L. D. Williams, Herbert S. Pigott, and Homer Harris.

1906: Charles McWilliams, keeper and surfmen, Washington Roberts, Matthew P. Guthrie, Melville Pigott, L.D. Williams, Herbert S. Pigott, & Homer Harris.

1907:Washington Roberts, acting keeper & surfmen, Leonard D. Williams, Matthew Guthrie, Edward H. Fulcher, Homer Harris & Monroe Gilgo

1908: Charles McWilliams, keeper and surfmen, Washington Roberts,L. D. Williams, Matthew Guthrie, Homer Harris, Monroe Gilgo, & Mitchell Hamilton.

1909: Charles McWilliams, keeper &  surfmen, Washington Roberts, L. D. Williams, Matthew Guthrie, Homer Harris, Mitchell Hamilton, & Simon Garrish.

1910: Charles McWilliams, keeper & surfmen, Washington Roberts, L. D. Williams, Matthew Guthrie, Homer Harris, Mitchell Hamilton, & Simon Garrish.

1911: Charles McWilliams, keeper& surfmen, Washington Roberts, L.D. Williams, Isaac O'Neal, Homer Harris, Mitchell Hamilton, & Simon Garrish.

1912: Charles McWilliams, keeper, & surfmen, Washington Roberts, L. D. Williams, Isaac O'Neal, Homer Harrism Mitchell Hamilton, Simon Garrish, & Monroe Gilgo.

1913 and 1914: Charles McWilliams, keeper, & surfmen, Washington Roberts, L. D. Williams, Isaac O'Neal, Homer Harris, Simon Garrish, Monroe W. Gilgo, Homer Harris, & Garry Bragg

**After 1914, the keepers were as follows:**

1915: Charles McWilliams

1916 & 1917:  Albert L. Barce

1918 - 1920: Mitchell Hamilton.

1921: Walter Yeomans, keeper and surfmen Samuel Williams, Robert L. Williams, Homer Harris, Walker Styron, Jesse Babb, and Whealton Gaskill. These men served until 1925.

In 1925, Joseph R. Emory was keeper and was followed by Roy Robinson who served from 1926-1931. G. H. Meekins was keeper in 1932 and from 1933-1934 E.G. Tillet served. G. L. Gray was the last keeper in 1935 and 1936. In 1937, the station became inactive and it was declared closed in 1938.

The station was reopened by the Coast Guard during World War II. Men patrolled the beaches and occupied the station.

After the war the station was once again vacated and in the 1950s the building was sold to a group who used the facility as a hunting lodge. They hired a man from Ocracoke to act as the caretaker. He was helpful to the island people, while he was there.

The Coast Guard Station still stands out so that the men at sea can see it and tell where they are when they get into trouble and need to come into the Ocracoke Inlet. I hope this station will remain as it is when the National Seashore Park Service takes over.

In 1922, the men that were in the station lived in little white houses close by the facility, as they were on call at all times. The station was painted white and the white cottages and green grass were so pretty here on the island.

They used large white horses with large hoofs to pull the cart up the beach on patrol. The large hoofs would keep them from sinking so far into the sand. I used to supply for some of the men at the station. In those days, if you were a seaman you could help out at the station.

Samuel Williams married my sister Neva while he was stationed in the Coast Guard station on Portsmouth. They lived in one of the little cottages near the station.

# Shipwrecks on the Beach

The *Ida C. Schoolcraft* came ashore off Core Banks in 1902. The *Vera Cruz* came ashore off Portsmouth Island in May 1903 with four hundred twenty-one men, women, and children aboard. Her main cargo was sperm oil. She also had on board the prettiest sheep that I have ever seen. They were large animals with the thickest, finest wool.

The people on Portsmouth Island opened their homes and took in these unfortunate people. It was a burden on the people, for they had to feed, clothe and find places for them to sleep until they could get help. One man died and was buried on the island.

The *D.D. Haskell* came ashore off Portsmouth Island in 1905.

The *John I. Snow* came ashore off the island in 1907. Her cargo was wearing apparel, all kinds, silk dresses, ladies undergarments, men's pants, shirts and even shoes. She had on board a complete hotel that they were carrying to be put up in New York. The first automobile that I ever saw was on the ship. It was more like a buggy than a car. It had side lights and large wheels.

Folks on the island salvaged most of the cargo and one of the men had a "endue" (this was a type of auction). My father bought the large white columns that were part of the hotel. He put them on our front porch. They were large and round and white and he used them to support the roof of the porch. The car was sold to Mr. Robinson of Washington, NC. Mr. Willie Gaskins bought the ship.

The *Melrose* came  ashore in 1908, she was a three-masted schooner. She came ashore of Core Banks about where the Pilentary Club house was, her cargo was salt. Her crew were

*When a ship went aground, Portsmouth families looked forward to "wrecking" (Photo courtesy of Outer Banks Museum, Manteo.)*

Portugese.  These poor people were pitiful, they looked about half staved and sick.

The *Luna* came ashore in July 1918.  Her cargo was lumber. She was a three-masted schooner.

The *Messenger of Peace* came into the Ocracoke Inlet.  She was boarded by government officials because she was loaded with whiskey.  She was enroute from the Bahama Islands to New York.  The men on the island had all of the whiskey they wanted to drink for quite a long time, this was in 1922.

The *Midgett* came ashore in the year 1952.  Her cargo was wheat and plenty of groceries, coffee by the cases.  You can see part of the wreckage ff the beach of Portsmouth on low tide.

Some of my family, some friends and I were on Portsmouth Island in the fall of 1961. We were spending a few days at our hunting lodge. We decided to set a net across one of the creeks that night to catch fish for our dinner the next day. We got up real early the next morning to go fish the net. While going toward the creek, we heard someone yell "hallo." We looked toward the beach and there was a man and woman coming toward the camp. Another man and woman had gone toward the Coast Guard station. Then we looked out to sea. To our surprise, we saw a two-masted sailing schooner sitting high and dry up on the high water mark. She was about fifty-feet long, enroute from the Virgin Islands to Buzzard Bay, Mass. They got off course and ventured too close the beach. It was a stormy night, so the waves washed her ashore.

They were scared people. They only had a flashlight for light, so they sat on the side of the boat all night. They were sure glad to see us. We gave them some dry clothes and helped them all we could. A man took them over to Ocracoke and they went home in a few days. Later, they got the schooner off before she sanded up. We never did see them anymore. I think this was the last schooner to come ashore off Portsmouth Island. Her name was the *Sea Hawk*.

To the Editor:
The worst storm and the longest in duration for this time of year in the memory of any man now living.  A grand total of 10 days, stormy days.

This storm struck the coast of Carolina, Sunday, November 25 and has continued bad with winds up to 70 miles per hour according to the weather station at Cape Hatteras. Extra high tides, three or four feet above normal now until the fifth day of December, 1962.  The outer banks have taken the worst washing ever, sand dunes washed and blown away and new inlets cut out through the banks here and there.  The outer banks cannot last much longer unless something is done by man; unless something is done and that pretty soon, there will be nothing left to build to.  I cannot describe the horrible, dreadful look of such devastation.  It is terrible to witness and I do wish that everyone in authority could have stood on the porch of our fishing and hunting lodge at the Sheep Island located on Portsmouth Island about three miles south of the Ocracoke Inlet and looked out on the Atlantic ocean  Tuesday morning, November 27, 1962.  Oh! What a site!

I hope and pray that something will be done and quickly. The outer banks certainly need immediate attention, and Portsmouth Island In particular.  The storm-batterd banks.

Just think, Portsmouth in 1815 or 150 years ago was the largest seaport in North Carolina and now there are just four people who live there year around. Oh! What changes have come about or taken place in 50 years, in my lifetime and remembrance.  What will happen in the next 50 years? God only knows.

Ben B. Salter, Portsmouth Island, N.C.

(This article appeared in the *Virginia News* in 1962.)

"The Sea and Ben Salter" ...*Virginia Reel*
By Jim Mays, Outdoor Editor
A Vanishing Island Cries Out for Help
Portsmouth Island, N. C.

*Dear Sir:*
*The worst storm and the longest in duration for this time of*
*year in the memory of any man living. A grand total of 10*
*days, stormy days. This storm struck the coast of Carolina*
*Sunday, Nov. 25, and continued bad with winds up to 70*
*miles per hour according to the weather station at Hatteras.*
*Extra high tides three to four feet above normal until the*
*fifth day of December.*

*The Outer Banks have taken the worst washing ever, sand*
*dunes washed and blown away and new inlets cut through*
*the banks here and there. The outer banks cannot last*
*much longer unless something is done and that pretty soon,*
*there will be nothing left to build on.*

*An ugly picture. I cannot describe the horrible, dreadful*
*looks of such devastation; it is terrible to witness and I do*
*wish everyone in authority could have stood on the porch of*
*our fishing and hunting lodge o the Sheep Island located on*
*Portsmouth Island about three miles south of Ocracoke Inlet*
*and look out on the Atlantic Ocean Tuesday morning, No-*
*vember 27th 1962, oh, what a sight.*

*I hope and pray that something will be done and quickly.*
*The outer banks certainly need immediate attention. Ports-*
*mouth Island in particular.*

*Just think, Portsmouth Island in 1815 was the largest sea-*
*port in North Carolina and now there are just four people*
*who live there and make it their home the year around.*
*Oh, what changes have come about or taken place in 50*

*years of my lifetime and remembrance.*

*What will happen in the next 50 years? God only knows.*
*Respectfully,*
*Ben B. Salter*

(By Jim Mays: For those who have never been to Portsmouth Island, it is a classic example of what can happen to a barrier island when the sea decides to calm its own. Like the rest of the outer banks of North Carolina, Portsmouth came from the sea and as Mr. Salter points out, will soon vanish back into the sea unless erosion is brought under control. On the maps, Portsmouth is the next island south of Ocracoke. It is a part of the isolated, lonely Core Banks of North Carolina. It has no telephones, no active Coast Guard station, and no access except by boat, or by landing a light plane on the beach. The sea laps unceasingly in the front yards of the four Portsmouth islanders who remain. Pamlico Sound laps at their back door. The dye is cast, it is now only a matter of time and the sea.

The same thing is also happening to the barrier islands off the eastern shore mainland. When they go, the sea will beat directly against the eastern shore and the consequences will be profound. You have only to see these great and beautiful stretches of sun-kissed, tide-washed sands to realize how very much they are worth saving for future generations.

(Mr. Salter is right. Portsmouth Island is a tragedy, and more tragedy is in the making.)

# Cemeteries on the Island

Out back of Miss Elma Dixon's and Marion Gray Babb's home is the Dixon or Babb Cemetery. There are five people and two parakeets buried there

**Arthur Edward Dixon**
Jan. 14, 1888
Oct. 31, 1945
*Weep not, he is at rest*

There is a Masonic emblem. He was a member of Bayboro Lodge.

**Lillian M. Babb**
July 30, 1896
Jan. 8, 1969
At Rest

**Nora Elizabeth Dixon**
March 5, 1892
Sept. 12, 1956
At Rest

**Elizabeth Pigott**
Aug. 28,1889
Sept. 12, 1960
At Rest

**Henry Pigott**
May 10, 1896
Jan. 5, 1971
*Gone But Not Forgotten*

The parakeets belonged to Mrs. Lillian Babb and Marion Gray. Dick died on May 4, 1961 and Pete died on November 9, 1960. They have nice little headstones made of cement about the size of a cigar box.

*(Editor's Note: Miss Elma Dixon and Miss Marion Gray Babb are also buried in this cemetery. They past away after this book was completed.)*

The Grace Cemetery is
located in the yard of the
Grace home.

**John K. Grace**
Born March 29, 1831
Died Sept. 8 1892

**Theresa Grace**
Born April 27, 1842
Died Jan. 14, 1912

*Farewell Dear Husband*
*Until I Meet You In Heaven*
**John B. Grace**
Born April 2, 1861
Died July 3, 1883

*Earth Has No Sorrow*
*That Heaven Can Not Heal*
**William Grace**
Born Nov. 11, 1867
Died Sept. 9, 1872

**Our Darling Boys**
In larger community cem-
eteries amid silver maple,
cedar trees, and rambling
pink roses you will find
these tombs.

**Dixon**
Beloved Husband & Father
**Harry Needam Dixon**
Sept. 10, 1889
Sept. 27, 1931
*Gone Home*

**Father**
**John B. Roberts**
Born Mar. 22, 1830
Died Mar. 19, 1894
*No Pain, No Grief,*
*No Anxious Fear*
*Can Reach Our Loved*
*One Sleeping Here*

**Mother-Martha**
Wife of George Dixon
Born Mar. 13, 1859
Died Mar. 4, 1914
*Weep not my children dear,*
*I am not dead but*
*just resting here.*

**Wilford D. Dixon**
Born Nov. 30, 1909
Died Nov. 23, 1922
Asleep in Jesus Blessed Sleep.

**James Styron**
Our Fair Son
James and Rebecca Styron

**Lida Dixon**
Sept.19, 1888
July 26, 1961
At Rest

**George Dixon**
Born Mar. 19, 1857
Died Nov. 24, 1919
*Don't weep for me dear, for*
*my toils are over. Someday*
*we will meet on the beau-*
*tiful shore.*

**Mary Helen**
Wife of Alfred Dixon
Born Dec. 22, 1876
Died Au. 22, 1927
*Sleep Mother sleep,*
*Thy toils are over, Well*
*how we loved thee, but*
*God loved three more.*

**George Rodnal Babb**
Born Oct 16, 1924
Died Oct. 18, 1924
Or Darling Baby

**Bettie Williams**
Juy 6, 1847
Sept. 11, 1927
Sleep dear one thy trials are
over, loved ones you'll meet
on the golden shore.

**Caroline**
Wife of William O. Williams
Born Nov. 4 1856
Died July 30, 1891

**Mary H. Parsons**
July 31, 1859
Died June 8, 1934
A Tender Mother and A
Faithful Friend

**Eugene**
Son of W. C. &
Mary E. Dixon
Born March 2, 1868
Died Sept. 23, 1888

*Blessed are the pure in*
*heart for they shall see*
*God.*

**Hugh Linwood Babb**
Born Aug. 19, 1912
Died Oct. 28, 912
*From Mother's Arms to the*
*Arms of Jesus*

*A large tomb with "Daly" at*
*the top.*

**William Daly**
Born in Dublin Ireland
June 2, 1844
Died in Beaufort, N.C.
Feb. 6, 1893
*Aged 49 years, 8 mos. & 4*
*days Farewell my wife and*
*children All, from you a*
*father, Christ doth call.*
*This marker bears a*
*Masonic Emblem.*

**Blanch G.**
May 10, 1897
July 21, 1927

**William T.**
June 15, 1887
June 29, 1948

How Desolate our Home
Bereft of Thee  There is a
Masonic emblem over
William T. at his feet Sgt.
Wm. Daly Sig. Corps, USA

**Our Mother Claudia**
Wife of William Daly
Born Mar. 19, 1857
Died Sept. 7, 1914
*Heaven now retains our
treasure, earth the lonely
casket keeps and her
children love to linger
where their precious
Mother sleeps.*

**Rita Johnson Gilgo**
Born Aug. 18, 1909
Died Oct. 15, 1911
Rita will sleep but not
forever There will be a
glorious dawn.  We shall
meet to part no never On
that Resurrection morn.

**In memory of Monroe Gilgo**
Mar. 26, 1882
Jan. 20, 1927
*We loved thee well, but
Jesus love thee best*
G I L G O

**Ronald G. Willis**
Born April 25, 1904
Died June   22, 1904
*Builded on earth to bloom
in Heaven*

A Bronze Plaque
**"Daisy"**
**Elizabeth Daly Gaskins**
Oct. 23, 1883
Feb. 22, 1926
**Elsie T. Roberts**
Born Oct. 15, 1858
Died Sept. 10, 1914
Thy memory shall ever be a
guiding star to heaven.

**William**
**Son of M. E. Roberts**
Born March 18, 1902
Died May 13, 1902
With Jesus in Heaven

**Mary E. Roberts**
Wife of Elsie T. Roberts
Born Aug. 24, 1878
Died Jan. 29, 1908
*A precious one from us has
gone A voice we loved is
stilled A place is vacant in
our home  Which never can
be filled.*

Behind Uncle Samuel
Tolson's home and just in
front of Mr. Will Willis', you
will find a cemetery with
thirteen graves.  They are
covered with bushes and
small trees. You have to
look for these graves.

Here are the graves in this cemetery

**Nancy Mayo**
Born Dec. 29, 1833
Died Jan. 26, 1906
Earth has no sorrow that
Heaven can not heal.

**James Mayo**
Born June 5, 830
Died April 18, 1900
Tho lost to sight,
to memory dear.

**Rachel Pigott**
Aug. 15, 1895
March 4, 1960
At Rest

**Benjamin R. Dixon**
1840 – 1924
An honest man is the
Noblest work of God.

In Memory of
**Maria Siewart**
Wife of Oliver Siewart
Born Nov. 14, 1816
Died Sept. 1, 1894
Blessed are the dead that
die in the Lord.

**George M. Dixon**
1867 – 1902
*Even from everlasting to
Everlasting thou art God.*

**Thomas Bragg**
Feb. 17, 1878
March 21,1968

**Jane A.**
**Wife of John V. Bragg**
Born June 22, 1839
Died Jan. 4, 1899
*Dearest Mother thou hast
left us, And thy loss we
deeply feel. But tis God
that has bereft us, He can
all our sorrow heart.*

*Community Cemetery*
*Photo courtesy of Frances A. Eubanks*

Susan J.
**Wife of Thomas S. Gaskill**
Born Dec. 11, 1840
Died Feb. 4, 1884
*Sleep Mother Sleep thy toils
are o'er. Sweet is thy rest
so oft needed before. Well
have we loved, but God
loved thee more. He's
called thee our Mother to
bright Heaven's shore.*

**Jane Ann
Wife of Alexander
Robinson**
Born Dec. 24, 1864
Died June 11, 1828
*Gone but not forgotten*

**James
Son of Alexander Robinson**
Born March 24, 1889
Died Feb. 20, 1909
*Sleep on dear James and
take thy rest, God called
thee home. He thought it
best.*

On the beach in front of the Coast Guard station, across the creek, covered over with sand and sage grass, are the graves of two Sea Captains. They lie beneath a blue marble tomb, the likes I have never seen before.

To the Memory of
**Capt. Thomas W. Greene**
of Providence, R.I. Died
Jan. 17, 1810 in the 32$^{nd}$
Year of his Age.

In thy fair book of life Divine, My God inscribed my name. That I may fill some humble place. Beneath the Slaughtered Lamb.

Beneath a white
marble tomb lies.
In memory of
**Capt. William Hilzey** who
Died Oct. 4, 1821. Aged 36
years, 2 months, 27 days.

*Far from my Native land My
spirit wings it's flight. To
dwell at God's right hand
with angles fair and bright.*

I can remember at least two more cemeteries on the island, one of them has long ago washed in the water. The other I cannot find, no one to keep the grass and bushes cut, soon these two will be gone.

Everybody on the island had a fig tree.
We enjoyed eating homeade fig preserves.

Dot Salter Willis'
## Fig Preserves

For a peck of figs.
Take stems off figs, but don't peel.

Place figs in pot with 4 pounds of granunlated sugar
and very little water.

Cook until figs are soft and the sugar has dissolved
into syrup. Some people added a slice of lemon.

Put in clean jars. Seal them. If we had wax we'd
use it on top of the preserves before sealing.

Pamlico Sound

Atlantic Ocean

Little Channel

Willis Creek

Beach Sand

Bill Salter's Creek

Tom Salter Camp

Sheep Island

Air Strip

Wallace Cemetery

John Styron's Creek

Old Salter Camp

Big Bushes

Ross Salter's

Newton's Point

Marsh

George Creek

Marsh Land

Bay Marsh Bay

Bay Marsh

Sand Grass

Dwarf Trees

Big Hill

Ben Dixon's Creek

School House Owned By Jean O. Burke

Cedar Trees

Ben Salter Home Moved From Sheep Island

Community Cemetery

Alec Robinson

George Dixon

Washington Roberts

Jody Styron & Tom Bragg

U.S. Post Office

Theo Salter's

Cemetery

Lionel Gilgo

Babb Home

Church

Grace Cemetery

Old Grace Home

Will Willis

Beach

Roy Robinson

Dave Willis

George R. Willis

Dixon Cemetery

Ed & Kate Styron's

Sarah Styron's

Old Brick Road

Henry Babb's

Gilford Dixon

U.S.C.G. Bldg.

Air Strip

U.S.C.G. Bldg.

Tom Gilgo's

Carl Dixon

Old U.S.C.G. Bldg.

Earl Mac

Henry Pigott's

Frank Gaskill

Doctor's Creek

Fish House

Coast Guard Creek

U.S. Coast Guard Station

Marsh

Haulover Point

Tin Bldg.

Haulover Slew

Casey's Point

Casey's Island

Ocracoke Inlet

Portsmouth Island          92          Short Stories & History

The land on Portsmouth Island was granted to Richard Lovat in 1738. It was deeded by Thomas Nelson in 1739 and in 1753 it was transferred to John Kersey. In 1753, the colonial assembly authorized the incorporation of a town. By 1756, seven people had purchased lots, including John Tweton, William M. Denham, Joseph Tweton, Charles McNair, Valentine Wade, John Campbell, and James Bun.

Fort Granville was built on an island in the inlet in 1758, but was decommissioned in 1764. The first academy was built in 1806.

1810 ..................387 people
1820..................382 people
1830..................411 people
1840..................400 people
1850.................. 505 people

*(residents 388, slaves 117, families 71)*

1860 ..................304 people
1870................. 341 people
1880..................221 people

By 1955, there were 18 people left on the island.

(In 1970, there were three, Henry Pigott, Elma Dixon, Marian Gray Babb.)

*The old livery stable at the lifesaving station.*
*(Photo courtesy of Burke Salsi.)*

*Portsmouth*

*was the*

*paradise of the*

*Outer Banks.*

– *Dot Salter Willis*